ISBN: 978-1-957922-59-1
Edition: November 2022

For all inquiries, please contact us at:
info@puppysmiles.org

To see more of our books, visit us at:
www.PuppyDogsAndIceCream.com

This book is given with love

To: _Alaric & Leyna_

From: _Manow Mary Ann & Ken_

Today, it's almost Christmas,
And there's so much left to do.
The dolls need braids, the balls need air,
The skates need laces, too.

His team's behind their schedule,
And, it's almost time to fly.
Though Santa's day is starting,
His blood pressure's running high.

When Santa's dressing in his suit,
It doesn't fit at all.
He finds a hole, the knee's worn through,
His belt feels far too small.

At breakfast, all the cookies,
Have been eaten by someone.
When he tries to drink the cocoa,
It's too hot and burns his tongue.

Now, it's time to check his sleigh out,
There's a storm that's blowing hard.
He can't see the barn or reindeer,
He can barely see the yard.

When he's exiting his cottage,
Santa slips and falls — ka-thump!
How can he be all merry,
When he's bruised his jolly rump?

His sleigh is scuffed and dirty,
And his reins are all entwined.
When Santa sits upon the cushions,
He gets mud on his behind.

In the stables, all the reindeer,
Lay about with tummy aches.
(Perhaps from all the cookies...
That those sneaky reindeer ate).

In the workshop, no one's working,
Not a single soul in sight.
The elves are all in the jacuzzi,
(After working through the night).

"Why on earth are you relaxing,
On our busiest of days?"
Santa asks the elves, who pipe up,
"Not until we get a raise!"

When it's time to make his milkshake,
There's no ice cream left to chug.
So, Santa stomps about the kitchen,
Letting out a "Bah Humbug!"

"For heaven's sake, now Santa!"
Mrs. Claus says hands on hips.
"You'd better tell me what is wrong,
I'm losing patience, quick."

"I can't find the Christmas spirit,
I've felt cranky all day through.
There's too much stuff that's going wrong,
There's too much left to do!"

Mrs. Claus says, "Dearest Santa,
Sure, some things have not gone right...
But even snowflakes sparkle,
When you see them in the light."

"We can't lose our Christmas spirit,
When a few things go awry.
Let's get some new perspective,
Before you head up in the sky."

"Though the snow can pile up quickly,
Just like problems in your day...
Every snowflake feels much lighter,
When you start to clear the way."

"Please list off all your problems,
We can talk through them out loud.
We can find the silver linings,
That surround your current cloud."

Santa takes a seat and grumbles,
"Well, today just isn't right.
From the moment that I woke up,
There were problems in my sight."

"My suit has holes, my belt won't close,
The sleigh is dirty, too!
I slipped on ice, I burned my tongue,
The reindeer....have the flu?"

As Santa details everything,
That have made him feel so mad...
His wife says, "Listen, Santa,
In new light, these aren't so bad."

"With the ice, we can make snow cones.
Cocoa's hot, without dispute.
The vet will check the sickly reindeer,
And I'll fix your belt and suit."

"We'll give the elves the raise they want,
In candy canes and cake!
It's true that they've been working hard,
And they deserve a break."

"Sure, your problems can all pile up,
And today, they came in bulk.
But remember, what's your purpose?
I know Santa doesn't sulk."

"You know, you're right, things aren't so bad,"
Says Santa with a sigh.
"These little things are fixable,
When seen with different eyes."

"Perspective helps me see the fact,
That these problems are all small.
And together we can help the world,
The reindeer, elves, and all."

Santa gives the elves the day off,
To relax and have some fun.
He will take them to Hawaii,
When the Christmas rush is done.

Mrs. Claus mends Santa's outfit,
Adds some flair to make it great.
The reindeer promise they will diet,
And keep cookies off their plates.

Soon the presents are all loaded,
And the sleigh is shining bright.
Santa calls out, 'midst the snowflakes,
"Merry Christmas, all! Goodnight!"

Claim your FREE Gift

 Visit:

PDICBooks.com/Gift

Thank you for purchasing

Grumpy Santa

How Santa Lost His "Cookies"

and welcome to the Puppy Dogs & Ice Cream family.
We're certain you're going to love the little gift
we've prepared for you at the website above.

CPSIA information can be obtained
at www.ICGtesting.com
Printed in the USA
BVHW021740221122
652360BV00005B/57